A NOTE TO PARENTS

When your children are ready to "step into reading," giving them the right books—and lots of them—is as crucial as giving them the right food to eat. **Step into Reading Books** present exciting stories and information reinforced with lively, colorful illustrations that make learning to read fun, satisfying, and worthwhile. They are priced so that acquiring an entire library of them is affordable. And they are beginning readers with an important difference—they're written on four levels.

Step 1 Books, with their very large type and extremely simple vocabulary, have been created for the very youngest readers. **Step 2 Books** are both longer and slightly more difficult. **Step 3 Books,** written to mid-second-grade reading levels, are for the child who has acquired even greater reading skills. **Step 4 Books** offer exciting nonfiction for the increasingly proficient reader.

Text copyright © 1994 by Kathryn Cristaldi
Illustrations copyright © 1994 by Denise Brunkus
All rights reserved under International and Pan-American Copyright Conventions.
Published in the United States by Random House, Inc., New York, and simultaneously
in Canada by Random House of Canada Limited, Toronto.

Library of Congress Cataloging-in-Publication Data
Cristaldi, Kathryn.
Samantha the snob / by Kathryn Cristaldi ; illustrated by Denise Brunkus.
   p.   cm. — (A Step 2 book)
SUMMARY: A young girl resents her new rich classmate until she gets to know her.
ISBN 0-679-84640-9 (pbk.) — ISBN 0-679-94640-3 (lib. bdg.)
[1. Jealousy—Fiction. 2. Friendship—Fiction. 3. Wealth—Fiction.]
I. Brunkus, Denise, ill. II. Title. III. Series: Step into reading. Step 2 book.
PZ7.C86964Sam 1994
[E]—dc20 93-19649

Manufactured in the United States of America 10 9 8 7 6 5 4 3 2 1

STEP INTO READING is a trademark of Random House, Inc.

Step into Reading™

Samantha the Snob

by Kathryn Cristaldi

illustrated by Denise Brunkus

A Step 2 Book

Random House New York

There is a new girl in my class.

Her name is Samantha S. Van Dorf.

The "S" stands for Snob.

The first time I met Samantha

she tried to shake my hand.

"How do you do?" she said.

"How do I do *what*?" I said.

Then I giggled.

Samantha stuck her nose in the air.

Samantha likes to wear fancy hats.

She wears them to class.

"Cool hat," says my friend Rita.

"I wish I had one."

Samantha tells Rita a secret.

Her hat is a designer original.

It is one of a kind.

That is a good thing, I think.

I would not want my friend

to look like a loony bird, too.

Today it is my turn to feed Walter.

Walter is our pet gerbil.

He is really cute.

First I get some lettuce.

Then I open the cage.

Uh-oh.

Walter jumps out.

He is on the loose.

I have to find him

before my teacher sees.

Suddenly I hear a shriek.

"Eeek! There is an ugly rat

under my desk!"

It is Samantha the snob.

She is standing on top of her chair.

"Who let Walter out?"

my teacher shouts.

Samantha sticks her nose in the air.

She points at me.

"Walter is not a rat," I say.

"But *you* are."

I will not call names.
I will n
I will r
I wi

My teacher makes me stay after school

I wave good-bye to my friend Leslie.

Leslie and Rita and I

are best friends.

Rita is in the coatroom.

She is trying on Samantha's fur coat.

She looks like a fat grizzly bear.

"Run!" I yell. "There is a bear

in the coatroom!"

Everyone laughs.

Except for the snob.

"I bet that coat cost

an arm and a leg," says Leslie.

Wow.

I would not give away my arm

or my leg to look like a big fat bear.

Leslie and Rita and I

take the bus to school.

We sit way in back.

We sing songs.

We wave to the people in the cars.

Sometimes I see the snob ride by.

She sits in the back
of a long, long car.
"I bet Samantha is watching TV
in there," says Rita.
"Cool!" adds Leslie.
"Big whoop-de-do!" I say.

One day in school

there is a pink card on my desk.

It has a picture of a cake on it.

There are balloons around the cake.

Oh, boy! I am going

to a birthday party.

I open the card.

It is a party all right.

A birthday party

for Samantha S. Van Dorf.

Everyone else is excited

about the party.

"Samantha says there will be

real pony rides," says Amy.

Big deal.

Pony rides are for babies.

"I heard she has an indoor pool!"

says Ricky.

So what.

I bet the water is ice-cold.

After school I play hopscotch

with Rita and Leslie.

"I am going to wear my red dress.

It has a lace collar," Leslie tells Rita.

"Where are you going?" I say.

Leslie and Rita look surprised.

"To Samantha's party," they say.

I cannot believe it.

My friends *want* to go

to the snob party.

At dinner I tell my mom and dad

about the party.

I tell them about the pony rides.

And the swimming pool.

"Samantha thinks she is so great

just because she is rich," I say.

"She is a snob."

"You should not judge a book

by its cover," my dad says.

I was not talking about books.

I was talking about Samantha.

On Saturday we shop

for Samantha's present.

I pick up a rubber snake.

It has ugly red eyes.

It wiggles in my hand.

I picture Samantha

opening my present.

She takes off the bow.

She unwraps the pretty paper.

Then she opens the box.

AAARGH!!

The snob faints.

She is out for the rest of the party.

It is the perfect gift.

Mom points to a doll.

The doll has blond hair.

Just like Samantha.

She has a turned-up nose.

Just like Samantha.

She is wearing an ugly hat.

I bet it is a designer original.

I hate it.

"How about this one?" Mom asks.

I smile. "Sure," I say.

"This one is perfect."

Perfect for a snob.

Tuesday is Samantha's birthday.

After school Rita and Leslie

come to my house.

Mom drives us to the party.

Rita and Leslie jump up and down.

They each have their bathing suits.

They have apples for the ponies.

I do not have my bathing suit.

But I do have something special.

It is my Captain Funnybone ring.

It squirts water from a flower.

I cannot wait to soak the snob.

At Samantha's house

I ring the doorbell.

A man opens the door.

He is dressed like a penguin.

I put my present in a huge pile.

There are kids running everywhere.

Some are wearing wet bathing suits.

They make puddles on the rug.

Samantha's mom stands
in the middle of the room.
Her dress sparkles.
She looks like a movie star.
"Game time, children," she says.
"Everyone, grab a partner."

I look around the room.

Leslie and Rita hold hands.

Ricky and Greg punch each other

in the arm.

Everyone has a partner.

Except me.

And the snob.

First there is the potato sack race.

On your mark. Get set. Go!

The snob runs one way.

I run the other.

We come in last.

It figures.

"Oh, well," says the snob.

I make a face.

37

Then there is the three-legged race.

The snob moves her left foot.

I move my right foot.

Plunk! We fall down.

I land on top of the snob.

"Sorry," I say.

"My fault," says the snob

from underneath me.

I give her a hand.

Next there is the wheelbarrow race.

On your mark. Get set. Go!

My sneakers are untied.

Whoops!

I trip.

We come in last.

"Are you okay?" Samantha asks.

She gives me a hand.

Now it is time for the egg race.

"I am good at this game,"

I whisper to Samantha.

On your mark. Get set. Go!

I walk across the room.

I am slow.

But the other kids are *too* fast.

They drop their eggs.

Not me.

"All right!" Samantha shouts.

Next it is her turn.

"Go slow," I say.

I make the thumbs-up sign.

That is for good luck.

My partner nods.

She crosses the finish line.

"Yahoo!" I yell.

We are the winners.

Samantha smiles.

She gives *me* the thumbs-up sign.

It is time for cake.

Samantha saves a place for me.

That is when I see her ring.

It is shaped like a flower.

It looks just like mine.

I hold up my hand.

She looks at my ring.

I look at hers.

Squirt!

We are both wet.

We are both giggling.

The cake comes out.

It says, HAPPY BIRTHDAY,

SAMANTHA SUE!

I smile.

"Samantha Sue," I say to myself.

That's a nice name

for a new friend.